CW01261823

Christmas at the Punk Rock Nursing Home

copyright © 2017 Marcus Blakeston

Second Printing 2018

This is a work of fiction. All names, locations, characters, events and incidents are the product of the author's imagination and any resemblance to actual persons, living or dead, is entirely coincidental. This includes Santa. Sorry kids, your parents were lying to you.

Christmas at the Punk Rock Nursing Home

Colin Baxter munched on a cheap regulation issue retirement home digestive biscuit while he browsed through the new messages in the Silver Punkers Community Forum on his entoPAD. Someone had mentioned the band Skrewdriver just over three months ago, and the resulting online argument still raged on. Colin had been among the first to post the standard 'Nazi punks fuck off' response, and it had all escalated from there, quickly degenerating into petty name-calling from both sides of the political spectrum.

He was bored with it all now, and just wanted it to end so everyone could talk about something else instead. He'd even started to feel nostalgic for the days when people argued about whether Green Day were punk or not, or whether Sid Vicious would have been the fattest Sex Pistol at their early 21st century reunion shows if he had lived long enough. But every time he thought the Skrewdriver post was finally as dead as Thatcher, up popped someone who must've been in a coma for the last few months and reignited it all over again.

"Pull a cracker with me, Colin."

Colin looked up from his entoPAD. Louise Brown stood before his armchair, a wide grin on her wrinkled, leathery face. A mass of pure white hair protruded from the top of a yellow paper crown with the words HAPPY FUCKING CHRISTMAS YOU CUNT written on it with a black marker pen. She held out a Christmas cracker she'd made from an empty toilet roll tube and the same yellow crepe paper she had used for her hat, and wiggled it before him.

Colin returned the smile as he put the entoPAD down on the arm of his chair and leaned forward to grip the proffered end of the cracker. Anything to escape the tedium of repeated posts basically just saying 'Commie' or 'Nazi' over and over again, with the occasional twerp pointing out that both Sid Vicious and Adam Ant used to wear Swastika armbands so it wasn't a big deal if Skrewdriver sang about the same sort of issues.

"Bang!" Colin and Luoise both shouted in unison as they tugged on the paper cracker and tore it in half.

Dave Turner, who had been staring into space the whole time, startled and spun in his armchair to face them.

"Eh? What's going on?" He fiddled with his hearing aid, which whistled constantly, as he peered myopically from Colin to Louise and back again.

"Nothing," Colin said, reaching inside the toilet roll tube to see what Louise had hidden within it. He pulled out another home-made paper crown and unfolded it on his knee. FUCK CHRISTMAS, Louise had written on it, I WISH IT COULD BE THATCHER DAY EVERY DAY.

Colin smiled to himself as he put the paper hat on his almost-bald, liver-spotted head and reclined back in his armchair. Louise knew him so well. While Colin didn't have anything against Christmas, and quite looked forward to it in his own way, it was nowhere near as much fun as the best day of the year. That glorious day on the 8th April when the elderly residents of the Punk Rock Nursing Home celebrated the death of that vile, horrible woman who had caused them so much misery in their youth.

Dave pulled a pair of jam-jar-bottom spectacles from his dressing gown pocket and put them on. He gaped around the retirement home lounge, taking in all the flame-proof tinsel and bunting draped over the framed album covers and replica punk fanzines decorating the walls as if he hadn't noticed it before, then peered at Colin's new hat.

"Is it Thatcher Day again, already?" he asked.

"No Dave," Colin said. "It's Christmas Eve. Thatcher Day isn't for another three and a bit months, yet."

"Oh." Dave's shoulders slumped. He sighed. "That's a shame."

Colin nodded in sympathy. "Yeah I know, but it won't be long now, and it gives us something to look forward to, doesn't it? Besides, tomorrow we'll get some proper grub, instead of the crap they usually give us."

"But we can still get Thatcher out and give her a good kicking, yeah?" Dave asked. "You know, just for something to do in the afternoon?"

Colin frowned. "Yeah well, we'd need to get her back off The Gestapo, first. He pinched her off us when he came back from the hospital last Thatcher Day, remember? Said she was a bad influence on us, and we couldn't play with her no more."

"Fucking bastard," Dave spat. "He's got no fucking right to take Thatcher off us like that."

Colin nodded. "Yeah I know mate, but what can we do about it? He's got her locked away in his office upstairs, and he just plain refuses to give her back."

"Well he'd better give us her back before the next Thatcher Day, or there'll be a fucking riot. You can't have Thatcher Day without Thatcher, can you?"

"We'll think of something, Dave," Louise said. "Besides, not everyone has a Thatcher, do they? And they still have a good time without one."

Dave scowled. "Won't be the same though, will it? It's traditional."

"Yeah well, so are Christmas crackers. So pull this one with me, and forget about Thatcher for now."

Louise held out another home-made cracker she had been hiding behind her back. Dave's hand shook as he reached for it and gripped the end with his gnarled thumb and forefinger.

"Bang!" Louise shouted as she whipped her arm back.

But the cracker just slipped out of Dave's fingers, still in one piece.

"You need to hold it tighter than that," she said, "or it won't work."

"I can't, it's me arthritis. I'm sure it's been getting worse over the last few months, I can't even shake me nob properly when I have a piss these days."

"Oh, poor you," Louise said with genuine sympathy in her voice. "Never mind, I'll do it for you."

"Yeah?" Dave grinned. "That'd be fucking great. I'll let you know next time I need one then, shall I?"

Louise frowned and shook her head. "I meant the cracker, you dozy bugger." She held the Christmas cracker in both hands and tore it in half herself ... "Bang!" ... then reached into the toilet roll tube, pulled out a paper hat, and placed it on Dave's head. "There you go. Proper festive, that is."

Colin leaned over to see what she had written on Dave's hat. He smiled.

"What's it say?" Dave asked.

"It says Santa is a fucking wanker," Colin replied.

Dave looked up at Louise. "How come?"

Louise shrugged. "Didn't you ever notice he gives all the rich kids better presents than he gives anyone else?"

Dave nodded. "Yeah, fair point."

"I blame Thatcher," Colin said.

"You blame Thatcher for everything." Louise laughed as she turned away and headed back across the retirement home lounge. She picked up another Christmas cracker from a pile of them on her armchair and held it out to Fiona Scott.

"Bang!" both women shouted.

Colin smiled across at them. Since they had all decided not to take the mysterious blue capsules the Workfare Assistants forced on them at medication time, the transformation in Fiona and the other residents had been remarkable. Where they used to doze in their armchairs all day, they were now active and alert. Even Frank Sterner, an original seventies punk now fast approaching his nineties, had an extra spring in his step as he shuffled around the retirement home lounge with his walking frame. All except for Tony Harris, who was now so weak and feeble he couldn't even stand without assistance, and was confined to a wheelchair in the corner of the room. The way he wheezed into his oxygen mask all the time, nobody expected him to last much longer.

"Talking of Thatcher," Dave said, "we really need to do something about liberating her from The Gestapo."

"Like what?" Colin asked.

"I don't know. Just get her back, somehow."

"Easier said than done, mate. You know what The Gestapo's like. Even if we somehow got into his office and rescued her, he'd only pinch her back off us as soon as he noticed she was missing."

Dave frowned. "Yeah. The fucking bastard would, at that. So if we can't give Thatcher a good kicking tomorrow, what are we going to do instead?"

Colin shrugged. "Dunno. Same as we do every other day, I suppose. Except with paper hats on our heads. Oh, and with better grub for dinner."

Frank Sterner wandered past, humming along to a Stranglers song playing softly through the retirement home lounge speakers. Colin smiled when he saw what Louise had written on his hat: XMAS WAS SHIT AFTER 1979, a reference to Frank always telling everyone that punk was better in the 70s, and nothing worth listening to was ever recorded after that decade. Not even the ones by his favourite bands when they reformed to take advantage of the growing nostalgia market when punks reached middle age at the turn of the century.

Colin picked up his entoPAD and looked down at it. The Skrewdriver post had attracted an extra thirty-two replies since he last looked a few minutes ago, and there was nothing new to keep it off the top slot. He sighed as he closed the Silver Punkers Community Forum and opened entoMOVIES to see if there was anything among that month's free titles worth watching. He settled on The Great Escape, something he used to watch every Christmas with his grandmother when he was young, and muted the device while he waited for the fifteen minutes worth of adverts to finish playing before the film would start.

After Louise had decked out all the residents on the far side of the lounge with paper hats, she picked up another two crackers and headed back over to Tony Harris and Greg Lomax. Tony was too weak to pull one, so she did it for him and placed the hat on his head, being careful not to dislodge his oxygen mask while she did so. When it was Greg's turn he reached out for the cracker with his right hand.

"Bang!" Louise shouted as the cracker tore in half.

"Bnnng," Greg said a second later. He spoke from the corner of his mouth with difficulty, the whole left side of his face drooped and immobile from a stroke he'd had several years earlier.

Louise helped Greg put on his paper hat, then returned to her armchair and sat down. Colin glanced at his entoPAD to see how much longer he would need to wait before he could watch The Great Escape. Another six minutes to go. The muted advert on the screen showed a topless young woman in boxing gloves repeatedly punching a man in a business suit in the face. *Had a work related injury?* the accompanying text said. *We can help with your compensation claim.*

The lounge door opened, and Dave nodded toward it.

"Ay up, what's he want?" he asked.

Colin looked across at the lounge doorway. The retirement home manager stood there and peered into the room. There was something odd about him, but Colin couldn't quite place what it was. Then he realised – the Thatcher-stealing bastard was actually smiling.

"I don't think I've ever seen The Gestapo smile before," Colin said. "Must've had his end away or something."

Dave laughed. "Maybe he's been shagging Thatcher. That's probably what he pinched her for all along."

"He'd better bloody not have been," Colin said, picturing it in his mind, "or he's buying me a fucking new one."

Beside the retirement home manager stood a new

Workfare Assistant, a young girl who looked so enthusiastic it could only mean it was her first day of real work since leaving school. She hefted an artificial tree with garishly coloured Sex Pistols baubles hanging from its branches into the lounge and stood it upright in the centre of the room. At the top sat a pure white fairy with its feathered wings outstretched.

"They can't even get that right, can they?" Dave said. "It should be Sid Vicious sitting up there, not a bloody fairy."

"Sid's dead, mate," Colin said with a hint of sadness.

Dave turned to face him, his eyes wide. "What? When did that happen?"

"Can't you remember, last year? He fell off the tree and Old Frank went and trod on him, snapped his arms and legs off."

"Can't he be fixed?"

Colin shook his head. "I think the Workfare Assistant we had back then must have chucked him in the bin, I haven't seen him since."

"Fuck. So first there's no Thatcher, and now there's no Sid Vicious? A fine bloody Christmas this is going to be."

"Yeah well, not much we can do about it, is there? And there's always the better grub to look forward to."

The retirement home manager took the young girl on a tour of the lounge, introducing her to each resident in turn. She seemed friendly enough, and took the time to chat with everyone before moving on. She even pulled one of Louise's remaining crackers, and laughed at the 'CHRISTMAS IS SHIT' message scrawled on the hat inside, although she did politely refuse to wear it. She was pretty, in a plain sort of way, with shoulder-length brown hair and an up-turned nose, and reminded Colin of his own daughter when she was that age. That same wide-eyed innocence at entering the grown up world of work for the first time, before jaded cynicism and boredom takes over and you wonder why you ever bothered.

"This is Colin Baxter," the manager said when it was Colin's turn to be introduced. The man's breath smelled of whisky fumes, and his voice had a faint slur to it, so he'd obviously been at the Christmas spirits. "I'd watch this one, if I were you. If there's ever any trouble, you can bet he's involved in it somehow." He jerked a thumb at Dave, sitting in the next armchair along. "Him and that one, there. That's Dave Turner, he's another trouble maker you need to watch out for. But they are both still active and can go to the toilet by themselves, so they won't take up too much of your time."

"Hello Colin," the girl said. "Hello Dave. I'm Tracy, I'm going to be looking after you from now on, and I'm sure we're all going to get along just fine."

"How do, lass." Dave nodded to her, then picked up his entoPAD and looked down at it.

"Aye up, Tracy," Colin said. "Pleased to meet you. Don't let the bastard grind you down, yeah?" he added with a jerk of his head at The Gestapo.

Tracy blushed. "I like your vest," she said, trying to change the subject. "It really suits you. Have you been living here long?"

Colin brushed biscuit crumbs from the front of his Sick Bastard thermal vest and held his dressing gown open so Tracy could see it properly.

"Thanks, I got it from the band when they played here last Thatcher Day. I've been here about four years I guess, but it seems a lot longer sometimes. I was lucky, they kept putting retirement age up every few years, so in the end I didn't need to move in here until I was seventy-five."

"It's eighty now," Tracy said. "They put it up again last year."

"Yeah? Does that mean I can go back home for another year, then?"

"It doesn't work that way, Baxter, and you know it," the manager said with a scowl. "There's nothing for you to go back to."

Colin ignored the man. That was something he didn't need reminding about; the day the state bailiffs came to evict him and move him into the retirement home was still as clear in his mind as if it had happened yesterday. Barricading himself in his downstairs flat had only delayed them by a few minutes before they swarmed in and seized everything of value to contribute to his future care costs. He'd been lucky to escape with Thatcher, if they'd known how much she was worth on entoBUY they would have grabbed her too.

"So what about you, Tracy? Have you always wanted to look after a bunch of old coffin dodgers like us, or were you just forced into it because nobody else wants to do it?"

"I always wanted to be a nurse, but I couldn't afford the study costs. This is the next best thing, and I'm really excited to have this opportunity to prove myself."

Colin wondered if Tracy was just saying that because The Gestapo was standing next to her, or if she really was that naive. He decided to play safe and not tell her she would be cast aside and replaced with another Workfare Assistant as soon as her six months placement was up. The manager would never waste money paying for staff when he could have an endless supply of free labour provided by the state.

"Well it's nice to meet you, Colin," Tracy said. "You too, Dave. And if there's anything you need, just come and ask me."

Dave nodded, without looking up from his entoPAD screen. "Will do, lass."

"Aye, thanks, Tracy," Colin said. After Tracy and the retirement home manager moved on to Tony and Greg, Colin turned to Dave. "She seems nice. Better than the other miserable bastards who end up working here, anyway. You could've at least made an effort to be friendly, get to know her a bit."

Dave shrugged. "No point, is there? She'll be gone within

a couple of weeks, the nice ones always are. The Gestapo will grind her down like he did the last one, and she'll be off."

"I bet you a biscuit she lasts the full six months."

"You're on," Dave said. "Easiest biscuit I'll ever make," he added. "You'll see."

Colin looked down at his own entoPAD. Another two minutes and The Great Escape would start. He pulled out his wireless headphones and put them on in preparation.

"That's Tony Harris," he heard the manager say. "He's pretty much a vegetable these days, so you'll need to change his clothes every now and again when he soils himself, but other than that he won't cause you any trouble."

"Fucking wanker," Colin said under his breath. How The Gestapo ever got to be manager of a care home for the elderly was beyond him. He didn't seem to care about anyone except himself. And since when did he ever show the new Workfare Assistants around, anyway? He usually just left them to figure it all out by themselves.

"And finally, this one is Greg Lomax. He had a stroke three years ago, and it seems to have left him brain damaged because all you ever seem to get out of him these days is gibberish. No idea if he can still understand us or not, but at least he can still go to the toilet by himself so you won't need to worry about any accidents."

"Irr cnn unnersnn evvrrrthng yrr crrnnt," Greg said. "Irrm nrr strrprd."

"See what I mean?" The retirement home manager turned to Tracy and smiled. "Complete gibberish. Now, if you will accompany me to my office, Miss Papper, I'll fill out a work schedule for you to follow."

* * *

Thirty-five minutes later, Tracy returned to the retirement home lounge with the medication trolley. She must have memorised every resident's name, because she took the correct medication from the trolley before she approached each one and handed them their dosage along with a fresh plastic beaker of water. She was also more trusting than any of the previous Workfare Assistants had been, because she didn't even wait to check if everyone swallowed their medication or not. Which made it a lot easier to just slip the blue capsules into dressing gown pockets for later disposal. Usually they had to pretend to take them, and then spit them out when nobody was looking.

Colin paused The Great Escape when it was his turn, then resumed it when she moved on to Tony Harris and shook him awake. It was coming up to the part in the film where David McCallum outlined his plan to dispose of the dirt from the escape tunnels, and it reminded Colin of how their own David, Dave Turner, had come up with a similar idea to dispose of the blue capsules after they found them impossible to flush down the toilet because of their buoyancy. It didn't involve socks, but the principle was the same – empty out the white powder inside them and scatter it all over the lounge carpet, ready to be sucked up by an army of cleaners on cleaning day, along with all the biscuit crumbs and dust. Then all that remained was to swallow the empty containers and nobody was any the wiser.

"Right then," Tracy said after the medication trolley had been wheeled away and put back in the storage cupboard in the hallway. "What shall we all do now?"

A few residents looked up and gaped at her in confusion, but most just carried on staring at their entoPAD screens. After medication, the Workfare Assistants usually just left them to their own devices for the rest of the day until it was time for bed.

"Come on, what's the matter with you all?" Tracy clapped her hands to get everyone's attention. "Let's play a game. I know, how about I Spy? Who wants to go first?"

A few more residents looked up from their entoPADs and gaped at her.

"Nobody? Okay, I'll go first. I spy, with my little eye ..." Tracy looked around the lounge in an exaggerated way, her index finger tapping the bottom lip of her open mouth ... "something beginning with—"

"We're not bloody kids," Frank Sterner grumbled as he hobbled past with his walking frame.

Tracy's cheeks flushed. "Oh. Okay, well how about a sing-song, then? You're not too old for singing songs, are you? Come on, it'll be fun."

A murmur of agreement spread around the retirement home lounge. Frank just huffed and continued his wandering. Colin paused The Great Escape once more, pulled the headphones off, and looked at Tracy with interest. His old friend, Brian Mathews, had told him all about the sing-along sessions at the retirement home he lived at, and it sounded like a lot of fun. But then again they did have Steve Snitch, the guitarist of the last remaining punk band Sick Bastard, living at their home.

"So what do you all want to sing?" Tracy asked.

"Bodies!" Louise Brown called out.

Everyone agreed. Even Frank grunted his approval as he stood stock still and reached into his dressing gown pocket for his entoPAD.

Tracy frowned. "I'm afraid I don't know that one, how does it go?"

Colin smiled. It was a good choice, and probably the only one that would make everyone happy. Never Mind the Bollocks was the one album that united each resident of the retirement home. It didn't matter if they preferred original 70s punk, UK82, anarcho, D-Beat or crust, the one thing they all agreed on was that the first Sex Pistols album was the absolute fucking dog's bollocks, and Bodies was the best song on it by a long mile.

Everyone except Tony Harris, who had drifted off back to sleep, opened entoTUNES on their entoPADs and scrolled through their playlists to find the required song. The opening bars of Bodies blasted out from dozens of speakers, all out of sync with each other and turned up to maximum volume, to create a cacophonous wall of noise that sounded like it came from a demented echo chamber set deep in the bowels of hell.

Then they all shouted the words to the opening lines, and Tracy's mouth dropped open. She waved her hands in the air.

"Stop it! That's a horrible song! Let's sing something nice instead! How about The Wheels on the Bus?"

But nobody was listening, they were too busy singing their hearts out. Frank Sterner leaned on his walking frame and bobbed up and down on the heels of his Sex Pistols slippers while he spat the words. Louise and Fiona screeched at the top of their lungs. Even Greg Lomax tried to join in, but by the time he'd managed to get the first line out everyone else was already on the second verse. Not that it mattered; he just skipped a few to catch up.

Tracy just stood there and shook her head all the way through.

"Frrr thrr nnn frr thar," Greg yelled. He sat upright in his armchair and waved his arms in the air, his fists clenched. "Frr irr orr nn frrr thrr frrnng brrrer!"

"Are you okay, Greg?" Tracy asked. She hurried over to him and placed the back of her hand against his forehead.

"Gerrerrf," Greg said as he batted her hand away. "Irrm jrst sinnnngnn."

The Sex Pistols track ended, and each resident's entoPAD blared out a different song as they continued with their own personal playlist. Colin's, which he had somehow managed to sort alphabetically by mistake and couldn't figure out how to undo, played Bodies in the Bath by The Astronauts. Dave's played State Pension by Sick Bastard, while Greg's, for some mysterious reason, blasted out Captain Sensible's Happy Talk. Everyone sang along with their own individual song, as if they either hadn't noticed, or just didn't care, what anyone else was singing. The combined noise was horrendous, and Colin placed his entoPAD speaker next to his ear to drown it all out while he made his own contribution to it.

Then the lounge door slammed back on its hinges and made everyone jump. The singing died down, just leaving the entoPADS to play to themselves.

"What the hell is going on down here?" the retirement home manager shouted. "Stop this horrible racket at once, before someone calls the police!" He stamped around the room and glared at each elderly resident until they prodded their entoPADs to silence the music, then marched over to where Tracy stood. "Miss Papper, I specifically told you not to get them excited. It's not good for their health, and it's my neck on the line if anything happens to them. So what have you got to say for yourself?"

Tracy's face went bright red. She bit her lip and looked down at her feet.

"I'm sorry Mr Smallcock, I just thought a nice song might cheer them up and put them in the festive spirit."

Colin snorted in derision when he heard The Gestapo's real surname for the first time ever. He wondered if his first name was Ivor. But at the same time he couldn't help feeling sorry for the young Workfare Assistant. None of it was her fault, even if she had come up with the idea in the first place.

"A nice song?" The Gestapo yelled in her face. "Is that your idea of a nice song? It's just a bloody noise, same as the rest of the crap they listen to all day. Why do you think I keep the volume so low on the speakers?"

Tracy's bottom lip trembled. "I ... I ..." Tears welled up in her eyes.

Colin picked up the walking stick leaning against his armchair and waved it at the manager.

"Fucking leave her alone, you cunt!" he growled. "It's not her fault. Like she says, she just wanted to cheer us up, which is more than you ever do. She didn't even pick the fucking song, we did."

"Stay out of this Baxter, how I discipline my staff is my

business, not yours."

"Bollocks. She's our carer, not yours, so it's up to us what she does. You don't even fucking pay her anything."

"Aye," Dave said. "Leave the lass alone, she's done nowt wrong."

"Yrrr," Greg added. "Frrr orrf nnn lrrrv errs alrrrn, yrr frrknn crrnt."

Frank hobbled over and shook the top of his walking frame. Louise and Fiona both shouted abuse from the far side of the lounge. Others murmured in agreement.

The manager frowned and shook his head. "Stay out of this, all of you. It's nothing to do with any of you." He turned back to Tracy. "Have they had their medication yet?"

"Yes," Tracy said. "I gave them it about fifteen minutes ago."

"Well they should have settled down for the day by now. I'm going to have to get on to the chemist, see if I can get them to increase the dosage for tomorrow otherwise it's going to be chaos. You stay here and calm them down while I sort it out." The manager turned and marched over to the lounge door. "And no more singing," he added just before he slammed the door behind him. "It's not good for them."

"Are you all right, Tracy?" Colin asked.

Tracy sniffed and wiped the tears from her eyes. "Yeah. Thanks for sticking up for me like that, I really appreciate it."

"No worries. He's a wanker, that bloke. That's why we call him The Gestapo."

Tracy gave out a short laugh.

"I don't suppose you've got a key to his office, have you?" Colin asked.

"No, why?"

"He's got something of ours in there, and we want it back."

"Sorry, I'd help you if I could, but I think he keeps the

key with him all the time."

Colin nodded. "Yeah, that wouldn't surprise me. Thanks anyway. And don't let him bully you, just tell him to fuck off out of it when he starts yelling at you. You're doing him a favour, remember? There's not many people who would want to work in a place like this for their food stamps when there's plenty of easier jobs out there."

Tracy smiled. "Thanks, I'll try and remember that the next time I mess up."

"You didn't mess up," Colin said. "You're just doing your job the way it was always supposed to be done. The others, the ones before you, none of them gave a fuck about us, all they cared about was getting their timesheet stamped so they could get their Workfare. You're different, and we don't want you to change just to suit The Gestapo."

Tracy blushed. "Maybe if we keep the noise down a bit in future?"

"Well we can try, but I can't make any guarantees. We like our music loud, we always have and we always will."

Colin put his walking stick down and picked up his entoPAD to resume watching The Great Escape from where he had left off. He offered Tracy a digestive biscuit, which she declined, then pulled one out for himself before passing the packet over to Dave.

Twenty minutes later, Colin knew how he was going to liberate Thatcher from The Gestapo's clutches. But he would need everyone's help to do it, and he didn't want Tracy to overhear any of his plans in case it got her into even more trouble. So he would need to keep it all to himself until late in the evening, after the Workfare Assistant had gone home and The Gestapo had finished his nightly prowl to check everyone was safely tucked up asleep in bed.

* * *

Colin woke up early on Christmas Day and reached for his entoPAD from the bedside cabinet, just like he did every other morning, to browse through the new posts on the Silver Punkers Community Forum. The male residents he shared the dormitory with were still fast asleep judging by the volume of noise coming from their open mouths, and he saw no point in waking them just yet. There would be plenty of time to meet up with the women and go over the plans for what he had dubbed Operation Thatcher one more time before they went into the lounge for breakfast and put it into action.

Placed on top of the entoPAD, Colin found a pink envelope and picked it up. He tore it open to reveal a Christmas card showing punk carol singers shouting at a flustered-looking Catholic priest, and stared at it in wonder. It was the first real Christmas card he'd received for over twenty years. People just didn't send things like that anymore, they sent electronic messages instead. He hadn't even thought anyone still made them out of actual cardboard. He opened the card up and smiled when he heard tiny disembodied voices shout 'Bollocks' and 'No future' over a sample loop of the opening bars of Pretty Vacant. An inscription inside read *Happy Xmas Colin, love Tracy.*

Colin sat up in bed and looked around the dormitory. Each bedside cabinet held a similar pink envelope placed on top of the owner's entoPAD, and presumably the women's dormitory would be the same. It must have cost Tracy a fortune to buy them all.

Colin stood the card up on his bedside cabinet and reached for his entoPAD once more. He prodded the screen with his gnarled index finger to wake the device up, then opened the Silver Punkers Community Forum. A post titled WAS SANTA A COMMUNIST OR A CAPITALIST? had taken the top slot away from Skrewdriver, which had been driven down to third place by someone asking about the best way to smuggle beer and cider into a nursing home. Colin shook his head while he read the suggestions provided, most of which were insane and would have no chance of working.

It reminded him of the last Thatcher Day, and the Sick Bastard gig he'd organised at the nursing home to celebrate the 30th anniversary. It was a day he would never forget for the rest of his life, just like the day when news of Thatcher's death first broke. Colin had been watching the BBC News Channel at the time, and he still remembered the absolute joy he felt as he punched the air and ran out into the street to tell his neighbours the fantastic news.

The entoPAD screen flashed, announcing an entoFACE request from user ANOK4UOK111. Colin accepted it, then fidgeted through the thirty second advert for medical insurance he could never hope to afford before Brian Mathews' wizened face grinned out at him.

"Colin, you cunt, how you doing? I noticed you was on the Silver Punkers, so I thought I'd give you a call and wish you a happy Christmas." Brian's hands shook so much that his image jerked around the screen like crazy.

"Ay up, Bri," Colin replied with a grin of his own. "Merry fucking Christmas, you old wanker. You and Brenda got any further with getting transferred over here, yet?"

Brian shook his head. "Nah, not yet, still working on it, but we'll join you there one day. Trouble is, ever since we told everyone about last Thatcher Day, and the beer and pizza after the gig, they all want to come with us in time for next year. Hang on, Brenda wants to say hello."

The image on the entoPAD screen flew around for a couple of seconds before settling on a frail-looking old woman who must have been sitting up in the same bed as Brian. She waved.

"Hello Colin, it's good to see you again."

Colin nodded. "Yeah, you too, Brenda. Merry Christmas."

"Merry Christmas. How is everyone over there?"

"Yeah, we're fine. Mostly, anyway. You know how it is, aches and pains and shit."

Brenda laughed. "Yeah, none of us are as young as we

used to be."

The image shot around once more as Brian turned his entoPAD back to face him. "So anyway Colin, you got anything special going on over there today?"

Colin glanced at the dormitory door and listened for any sign of The Gestapo lurking out in the hallway and eavesdropping in on his conversation with Brian. He couldn't hear anything, but decided to play safe and put the entoPAD microphone next to his mouth as he whispered, "Yeah, today's the day we get Thatcher back from The Gestapo, but keep that to yourself." He moved the entoPAD back to arm's length and said in his normal voice, "No, not really. Just the usual crap, but with better grub and paper hats. How about you?"

"Yeah, the same. We'll probably just veg out, maybe watch Breaking Glass or something on the big wall screen. Then later on we'll have a sing-song with Steve Snitch on his guitar, then go to bed."

"Sounds like a good plan," Colin said. "Singing's been banned over here."

"How come?"

"The Gestapo doesn't like it."

"Fuck him, he can't stop you singing if you want to."

"Yeah, I know, but we've got a really good Workfare Assistant at the moment, she only started yesterday, and we don't want to get her in trouble in case The Gestapo gets rid of her before the full six months is up."

Brian nodded. "Yeah, that makes sense. There's not many good ones around, so when you get one you like you need to hold onto them as long as you can. The one we've got now is a right miserable bastard, I can't wait until he's replaced."

"You want to make it as difficult for him as you can," Colin said. "That's what we do when we get one we don't like. Pretend to be deaf when he talks to you, and always do the opposite of what he tells you to do. They think we're all senile anyway, so it doesn't hurt to play the part now and again. If you make their job hard enough they'll just think 'fuck it' and go back to the Workfare and ask for something easier instead. Like herding cats or whatever."

Brian gave out a rasping laugh. His image on the screen jerked around even more. "Sounds like a good plan. What do you reckon, Brenda?"

"Fuck, yeah," Brenda said from off screen. "We should get together and organise something like that too."

"Anyway, gotta go," Brian said. "Just got time for a quick fumble with me bird before we go down for breakfast. See you later, Col."

"Yeah, see you, Brian. Bye, Brenda."

"Bye, Colin."

Brian forgot to disconnect the video call, and Colin was treated to a bouncing view of the ceiling while he heard rustling sounds and wet smacks and moans. He disconnected it himself, and waited for the thirty second advert to play out before the device relinquished control back to him.

The other occupants of the dormitory were starting to wake up from all the noise he'd been making. All except for Dave Turner, who snored away oblivious to everything without his hearing aid. Colin decided to give him another five minutes, then poke him with his walking stick if he wasn't awake by then. They needed to get the plan sorted before The Gestapo started prowling around.

* * *

After Thatcher Day, Christmas dinner was always the highlight of the year at the Punk Rock Nursing Home. Instead of boiled cabbage and watery soup they got chicken with stuffing for the carnivores, and Quorn roast with crushed mixed nuts filling for the herbivores. Both dishes came accompanied with potatoes and parsnips roasted in vegetable oil, and boiled peas, sprouts and carrots, topped off with either onion or beef gravy. And instead of the usual water to wash it all down, they got a beaker of orange squash each, with as many top-ups as they wanted.

It all arrived in a catering van at just after mid-day, and each resident took up their seats at the huge dining table laid out on one side of the lounge while they waited for Tracy to dish it all up for them and prepare the orange squash. The Gestapo sat at the head of the table, wearing a blue pin-striped suit and clutching an upright knife and fork in his hands as he told Tracy to hurry up and get on with it. Tony Harris sat at the opposite end in his wheelchair, next to where Tracy would sit so she could spoon-feed him pre-chopped food between gasps on his oxygen supply. Colin sat near the middle, between Greg Lomax and Dave Turner, with Louise Brown and Fiona Scott sitting opposite him.

In the background, the volume turned down even lower than usual, a punk version of the traditional Christmas carol Oh Come All Ye Faithful by the American band Bad Religion played through the lounge speakers. Colin would have preferred Hard Skin's Ding Dong Merrily Oi Oi, but it had been Tracy who programmed the day's playlist and she said if she had to listen to Christmas punk songs all day it would need to be ones that she knew the words to, and she had to vet them all in advance in case there was any swearing. Like a lot of young people, she seemed to have got it into her head that the older generation were offended by such things. Like fuck they were.

Tracy looked flustered as she carried the full dinner plates in, two at a time, and plonked them down on the dining table before returning for more. Louise offered to help, but Tracy said she could manage. Everyone waited patiently until they had all been served and Tracy joined them before tucking in. Except for The Gestapo, who started on his as soon as his plate hit the table. Colin watched him shovel it all down as if he wanted to get his annual obligation to spend time with the old folks he was supposed to be caring for over and done with as quickly as possible. Operation Thatcher depended on him hanging around long enough to need a refill of orange squash, but he hadn't even touched the one he had yet. Drastic measures were needed if this was going to work. Colin leaned on his walking stick and grunted as he pushed himself up onto his feet.

"Where are you going, Colin?" Tracy asked as she forked a soggy sprout into Tony's mouth. "Is something the matter?"

"I need a piss."

The retirement home manager glared at him. "Couldn't you have done that before you sat at the table?"

"I didn't need one then."

"Do you need me to help you get there?" Tracy asked.

"No, it's okay, I can manage. You carry on with your dinner, I won't be long."

Colin hobbled along behind the seated residents, placing one hand on each shoulder for additional support as he made his way closer to where The Gestapo sat chewing a huge chunk of roast chicken he'd just popped in his mouth. When he reached him he pretended to stumble and reached out for the dining table to stop himself falling, knocking the manager's orange squash over in the process. The beaker poured its contents all over the table, some of it spilling into the man's lap. He shot up from his chair, a look of absolute fury on his face, and grabbed his wet crotch.

"For god's sake Baxter, now look what you've done. I'll have to go and get changed now."

"Sorry, Mr Small Cock," Colin said, deliberately leaving a short gap in the middle of the man's surname. "It was an accident, honest. Don't worry, I'll pour you a new one." He reached for the large glass jug Tracy had filled everyone's beaker from.

"Just leave it Baxter, you'll only spill it everywhere. Let Miss Papper do it, that's what she's here for."

The Gestapo stormed out of the room. Tracy started to

rise to her feet, but Colin waved her down.

"It's okay, Tracy, I'll do it. You just enjoy your dinner in peace, don't take any notice of what he says."

"Well if you're sure it's not too heavy for you?" Tracy hesitated before sitting back down.

"Yeah, no worries, I can do this."

Colin picked up the upturned beaker and reached into his pocket for the blue capsules he'd collected from the other residents earlier in the day. He used his body to shield his hands from Tracy's line of sight while he pulled four of them apart and dropped the white powder into the beaker, then filled it up with orange squash and put it down next to The Gestapo's dinner plate. There had been some argument the night before about what the ideal dose should be. Not enough, and it wouldn't work. Too many, and it might kill him and they would all get in trouble for it. If they knew what the blue capsules were called they could look up the correct dose on the entoWEB, but without that information all they could do was guess at how many they would need.

Nobody had argued against such drastic measures. After all, as Louise pointed out, The Gestapo had been feeding them those same drugs twice a day, every day, for years. Just to keep them all docile and give himself an easy life. So it was time the bastard found out what it was like being on the receiving end. They eventually all agreed that if two capsules made you drowsy, then four ought to be enough to send someone to sleep for a few hours. And if it wasn't, they could always add more later.

With phase one of Operation Thatcher completed, Colin returned to his seat and took a sip of his own orange squash.

"I thought you needed the toilet?" Tracy asked with her head cocked to one side.

"False alarm," Colin replied. He winked across the table at Louise. She smiled and winked back, then forked a slice of Quorn roast dripping with onion gravy into her mouth.

Colin tucked into his own dinner while he waited for The Gestapo to return and take his medicine, so phase two could begin.

The manager returned in a fresh suit five minutes later and sat down in his seat at the head of the table to resume his dinner. Colin watched as he took a gulp of orange squash, then pulled a small bottle of vodka from his inside jacket pocket and filled the beaker up to the top. He wondered if the alcohol would affect the drugs or not, then decided it wouldn't really matter either way. If four capsules wasn't enough, he could always figure out some way of getting more into him.

Dinner continued with a hubbub of conversation as everyone reminisced about the old days when families would always get together and forget their differences for one day each year. How their grandparents were included in everything, not just forgotten and left to rot in a nursing home like they are now. Stuffing their faces with huge amounts of food, then drinking vast quantities of alcohol while they watched James Bond on the telly.

Colin kept an eye on The Gestapo, growing more and more anxious by the minute. So far the manager hadn't shown any signs of fatigue, despite having drunk several beakers of vodka and orange. It looked like he was going to need a larger dose of whatever was in those blue capsules after all. But that was easily enough sorted. He'd just help Tracy serve up the pudding, and sprinkle a few more into the bastard's custard.

Tracy cleared away the plates after everyone had eaten their fill of Christmas dinner. The manager belched and poured himself another vodka and orange, then downed it all in one long gulp. His eyes were glazed and vacant as he swayed from side to side in his seat. Colin glanced at Louise. She smiled and rubbed her hands together. The drugs were working after all.

The manager's head bowed into his chest, then he toppled forward and his face smacked into the table before he rolled off his chair and fell in a heap on the floor.

"Oh my god," Tracy yelled as she rushed over to him. "Are you okay, Mr Smallcock?"

"Let me take a look," Louise said, "I used to be a nurse."

This was a lie, of course, and all part of Operation Thatcher. The only job Louise had ever had in her life was as a shop assistant in the local Tesco before all the staff were replaced by robots and self-service automatic trolleys that debited your bank account each time you placed an item inside them. But Tracy didn't know that, so she stood back and let Louise crouch down to examine the unconscious retirement home manager.

"He'll be okay," Louise said after prodding him a few times with one hand while she slipped a bunch of keys from his jacket pocket with the other. "He must have drunk too much vodka, he just needs to sleep it off for a few hours and he'll be right as rain." Louise closed her fist around the keys and straightened up with a grunt.

"We can't just leave him lying there like that," Tracy said. "We should at least put him in his bed or something."

"We'd never get him up the stairs," Colin said. "Like Louise says, he'll be fine once he's slept it off. You'll need to keep an eye on him though, in case he spews up or something and chokes on it."

Tracy's mouth dropped open. "Oh my god, I never thought of that. Do you think I should phone an ambulance instead? I mean, I've got all of you to look after, too."

Colin shrugged. "It's up to you, but I don't think he would thank you for it if he lost his job for being drunk in charge of an old folks' home."

Tracy's eyes widened. "Could that happen?"

"Dunno. Maybe. Or maybe he might just blame it all on you, it wouldn't surprise me."

"So what should I do? Phone the Workfare and get them to send someone else to help out?"

"Just leave him there and watch him until he wakes up. If you tell the Workfare what's happened, that might get you both in trouble too."

"But what if something happens to the rest of you while I'm stuck here?"

"Like what?" Colin pointed over to the armchairs lining the walls of the room. "We'll just be over there, if we need you we can yell, then Frank or whoever can watch him for a bit while you sort it out."

"Okay, that makes sense. Yeah, let's do that."

Tracy sat down in the manager's dining chair and bit her lip while she leaned forward and stared down at his unconscious body. Colin, Louise, Fiona and Greg used the opportunity to slip out of the lounge without her noticing, then made their way down the corridor and up a flight of stairs to The Gestapo's office. Louise tried two of the keys before she found the right one to open the lock and pushed the door open.

Colin stared inside at the spacious office. It was almost as big as the dormitory he shared with eight other residents, and he'd never seen anything like it before. A huge screen took up an entire wall, displaying a pattern of swirling colours. Set before it was a solid oak desk and a black leather executive chair on castors, and covering the floor was the most luxurious fitted carpet he'd ever seen.

Colin slumped into the chair to give his aching legs a rest after all the exertion of climbing up the stairs, and reached out for an over-sized entoPAD placed on the desk, which was the only thing on there. It was huge, at least four times the size of a normal entoPAD, and when he prodded it the screen on the wall came to life and mirrored its display. As well as the usual entertainment options – entoTUNES, entoMOVIES, entoPLAY and entoBOOKS – was something called entoOFFICE. He dabbed its icon with interest to see what it was, while the others searched the room for Thatcher.

"Shrr nrr hrrr!" Greg said.

"Well she has to be somewhere," Fiona replied.

"Let's try his bedroom, maybe she's in there," Louise said.

They all trundled out of the office, but Colin barely noticed. He'd found a file labelled 'annual accounts' and was busy skimming through it trying to decipher all the various headings and lists of numbers, some positive and some negative. None of it seemed to add up at all. There were items listed under 'entertainment' that just didn't make any sense. A premium subscription to entoMOVIES, when he knew for a fact they only had the basic free package. Dozens of replacement entoPADS, certainly more than he could remember needed replacing after someone sat on them or trod on them. And something called 'visiting entertainers' that had an entry on the last Friday of every month. The cost of food and drink seemed way over the top too, considering the cheap crap they were fed each day. But it was the staffing costs that really caught his eye. According to the file, there were three full time carers being paid an above average salary each. Other than the cleaning staff who came once a week, and an endless rotation of Workfare Assistants, Colin had never seen any of them the entire time he had been living there. So where were they?

"Colin, we need you," Louise called out from the office doorway.

Colin spun in the chair to face her. "Here, Louise, come and have a look at this, see if you can make any sense of it. I reckon The Gestapo might be ripping the government off."

"Never mind that now, we've found Thatcher."

"Where is she?"

"She's on top of a wardrobe, but we can't reach her. We need your walking stick."

Colin pushed himself upright and followed Louise to the manager's bedroom. Like the office, it was huge and no expense had been spared in furnishing it. A solid oak dressing table stood beside the biggest and most comfortable-looking bed he had ever seen. Greg and Fiona sat on the edge of it, while a silk dressing gown with a dragon pattern and matching silk pyjamas lay spread out behind them. A huge pair of speakers, much bigger than the ones in the lounge downstairs, stood either side of the wall opposite the bed, with another large screen mounted between them. There was even a walk-in bathroom, with a toilet and bidet, and a Jacuzzi big enough to fit three people into it.

Louise pointed at a solid oak wardrobe on the far side of the room. Colin followed her gaze, and stared into the wide, blood-shot eyes of Thatcher. Her long, pointed nose hung down over the edge of the wardrobe, hiding her gaping red mouth.

"Cnn yrrr rrish hrr wthh yrr wrrnnnkistrrk?" Greg asked.

"I'll try," Colin said.

He hobbled over to the wardrobe and reached up with his walking stick while he stood on his tiptoes. The rubber end of the stick wavered in the air several inches short of the tip of Thatcher's nose. He leaned his chest against the wardrobe door while he tried to stretch higher, grunting with the effort.

"It's no good," he said, shaking his head. "She's too high up. I can't reach her."

Colin lowered the walking stick and leaned on it while he wheezed for breath. They were so close to liberating Thatcher, but she might as well be ten miles away for all the good it did them. All that effort, all that planning, and it had been for nothing. Colin slumped down on the bed next to Greg and sighed.

Greg patted him on the shoulder. "Nvvrrr mnnnd Colnnn, yrr trridd yrrr brrsst."

"I've got an idea," Louise said. "Wait there."

Colin, Greg and Fiona stared up at Thatcher while they waited. She stared down at them, as uncaring as she had ever been.

Louise returned fifteen minutes later with Frank Sterner's walking frame and set it down beside the wardrobe. She turned to Colin and grinned.

"Here you go, problem solved. It cost me a whole packet of biscuits to borrow it, mind, so I hope you'll all chip in some of yours towards it."

"That won't be gig enough," Colin said. "It's shorter than my stick, and even if it wasn't it would be too heavy to lift that high."

"It's not for lifting, it's for standing on."

"Eh?"

Louise pointed at the horizontal bracing bars holding the frame together. Like the frame itself, they were of an aluminium tubular design, set about twelve inches from the ground.

Colin shook his head. "That'll never hold my weight."

"Maybe not," Louise said, "but it will hold mine. Now let's hurry up and get this done, before The Gestapo wakes up, or Tracy notices us missing and comes looking for us."

Fiona and Greg held the walking frame steady while Colin helped Louise climb onto it. She clung onto the rubber handle grips with both hands while she found her footing on the front bracing bar, then reached out for Colin's walking stick. Colin handed it to her and stepped back to watch. The walking frame tilted onto its back legs a couple of inches as she let go of the grips and reached up to slap her left hand against the wardrobe door. Greg and Fiona braced themselves against it to stop it from toppling over. Louise raised the walking stick in her right hand. Colin directed her where it needed to go, right under Thatcher's nose.

"Left a bit. No, not that far. Back a bit. There, that's it. Go!"

Louise thrust up with the walking stick. Thatcher's head reared up, then dropped down again with a faint thud after the end of the stick slid off. A cloud of dust billowed up around her. Her nose protruded over the edge of the wardrobe a little bit more than it had before.

"It's working," Colin said.

Colin gave Louise directions again, and this time Thatcher's entire head lolled over the side of the wardrobe.

"Nearly there," Colin said. "Just one more time should do it."

Under Colin's guidance, Louise managed to fit the tip of the walking stick into Thatcher's gaping red mouth. She swung the stick away from the wardrobe with a grunt. Thatcher sailed through the air, her flaccid, naked body billowing out like a horrific flag as she flew straight at Colin.

"Ahhhgh!" he shouted as he tried to raise his hands to ward her off.

But he was too slow. The back of Thatcher's head smacked into Colin's face with a whump, causing him to stumble back against the edge of the bed. He gagged at the foul, dusty taste of her in his open mouth as her deflated body continued its forward momentum and wrapped itself around his entire head. He grabbed at her and tried to wrestle her from him, but her latex body seemed to have attached itself to the back of his bald head and wouldn't budge. His heart raced in panic. He couldn't breathe! His muffled cries for help must not be loud enough for anyone to hear because nobody came to his assistance. He twisted from side to side as he wrestled to free himself from Thatcher's clutches, but it was to no avail. Her grip around his head was just too strong for him. He felt himself weaken through lack of oxygen and sat down on the bed before falling onto his back with his arms splayed. The bed was so soft he bounced up and down on it for several seconds, Thatcher's head bouncing off his face each time, allowing him a split second to gasp for breath before she smothered him once more.

Then, just as he thought he was going to black out forever, the bed bounced once more and Thatcher's head was lifted from his face.

"Are you okay Colin?" Louise asked. She peered down

at him, her wrinkled face a mask of concern as she straddled him on the bed.

Colin lay beneath her, unable to reply as he gasped and wheezed, his heart still pounding in his chest like a Discharge drum solo. But despite it all, he couldn't help smiling. That would have been the ultimate punk rock death – murdered by Thatcher. But he had survived despite all the odds, just like he had survived in the 1980s during the real Thatcher's reign of terror.

After Colin's breathing and heart rate returned to normal, Louise helped him back onto his feet. He embraced her bony body in gratitude and planted a wet kiss on her gummy lips.

"Thank you," he said.

Louise's eyes widened as she stared at him for a second, then she grabbed the back of his head and pulled him in for another lingering kiss. Her tongue darted into his mouth and one hand drifted down to squeeze his arse, and this time it was Colin's eyes that boggled.

"Grttrr frrknn rmmm," Greg said.

Fiona laughed. "Well it's about fucking time you two got together, but can you do that later? You wouldn't want Tracy walking in on you when she comes to find out where we've gone." She took hold of Frank Sterner's walking frame and dragged it out of the bedroom behind her.

Colin reluctantly disentangled himself from Louise's grasping hands and turned to face Thatcher. She lay slumped across the bed, her arms and legs twisted at odd angles. Strips of flesh-coloured rubber patches covered the many puncture wounds she had suffered over the years of abuse her body had received. He gripped her by her webbed feet and dragged her off the bed, then spun her round and tossed her at the bedroom door. Greg kicked her through it, and mumbled to himself as he continued kicking her down the hallway toward the stairs.

Louise slipped her hand into Colin's. "Come on, then," she said, and led him out of the room before locking the door behind them.

Colin paused outside The Gestapo's office when he remembered he had left the nursing home's accounts file open. If the manager saw it he would know someone had been snooping in there. He stared again at the columns of figures displayed on the wall, not quite understanding what he was looking at, but sure there was something dodgy going on. He asked Louise if she could make any sense of it all, but she just shrugged and shook her head. Colin decided to take several photographs of the screen display with his entoPAD before putting everything back the way it had been before. Maybe if he posted the pictures on the Silver Punkers Community Forum someone might be able to explain it all for him.

Back downstairs in the lounge, Tracy still sat at the dining table looking down at the retirement home manager's unconscious body. Colin checked the man's chest was still rising and falling before he picked Thatcher up from where Greg had left her next to the Christmas tree and used Tony Harris's spare oxygen cylinder to inflate her through the valve that formed one of her nipples. Her body crackled as it ballooned out and took shape. Her latex arms rose up and reached out like a zombie hungry for human flesh. A cheer rang out from the other residents as they watched on from their armchairs.

Tracy looked up to see what was going on. Her eyes darted around the room, then settled on Thatcher's naked body. "What on earth is that you've found, Colin?"

Colin disconnected the oxygen cylinder and pushed Thatcher's nipple valve back into place to stop her from hissing at him. He positioned her in front of him and waved her outstretched arms at Tracy.

"I am The Thatcher," he screeched in a high-pitched voice, "and I have returned from hell to wish you all a miserable Christmas."

Dozens of geriatrics struggled out of armchairs and headed over brandishing walking sticks and cushions. It was the cue they had all been waiting for.

"It's vile and horrible, that's what it is," Tracy said.

Colin grinned. He couldn't agree more, but it was no more vile and horrible than the real one had been. He spun Thatcher round in his arms and punched her in the face, sending her somersaulting across the room into the arms of the other residents. He'd learned from experience not to get in the way while they set about her mob-handed.

Tracy watched it all with her mouth hanging open. It was obvious she'd never seen anything like it before.

"Settle down," she kept saying, "you'll do yourselves a mischief."

But nobody was listening, they were too busy having fun. Fluffy slippers thudded into Thatcher's prone body from all directions. Walking sticks whacked her in the crotch. Cushions thudded into her face. Frank Sterner leaned on his walking frame while he stamped on her legs.

After a matter of minutes their energy started to flag, and one by one the residents returned to their armchairs exhausted and happy. Colin limped over to Thatcher, surprised she hadn't suffered any new punctures from the beating, and kicked her across the room to where Tony Harris sat in his wheelchair.

"Here you go, mate," he said as he held Thatcher up before the frail, wheezing man.

Tony raised a shaking fist and tapped it against Thatcher's forehead. Colin jerked her head back as if it had been a killer punch, then threw her on the floor.

"And it's a knockout! The Thatcher has been defeated once more."

Tony grinned behind his oxygen mask. Colin booted Thatcher over to the Christmas tree. Dave Turner stood her upright next to it, and Louise put one of her paper hats over her head. THATCHER'S DEAD, she had inscribed on it.

"Was there a point to all that?" Tracy asked with a smile on her face.

Colin just grinned back shrugged. Maybe he would explain it all to her if she stuck around long enough to still be there on the next Thatcher Day. After returning the keys to the retirement home manager's pocket he slumped down in his armchair, took out his entoPAD, and opened the Silver Punkers Community Forum so he could post the photographs he had taken of the accounts file. Maybe if he could find out precisely what The Gestapo was up to it might give them all a bit of leverage over him. Maybe even enough to force him to keep Tracy on full time, and buy in some proper food and better biscuits. Maybe even make room for Brian and Brenda to move in. Or at least let them keep Thatcher in the lounge as a permanent punch bag to take out their frustrations on.

While Colin waited for someone to decipher the retirement home's accounts for him, Louise wandered over with something wrapped in yellow crepe paper. She held it out to him and smiled.

"Happy Christmas, Colin."

"Oh," Colin said. "Thanks. I didn't get you anything, though."

"Don't worry, we can share it."

Colin unwrapped the paper and found a round blue pill inside. He held it between his thumb and forefinger as he stared at it, then looked up at Louise.

"What is it?"

"Viagra. Fiona's got a stash of them left over from before her husband died, she says she doesn't need them anymore so we can have as many as we want. They're pretty old, but they should still work okay. Just like us, eh? I thought we could try one later, after everyone's gone to sleep."

Colin grinned. This was turning out to be the best Christmas he'd had for a long, long time.

Stabby Abby in . . .
A Very Stabby Xmas

Christmas Eve in the Black Bull is fucking mental, yeah? It's like every fucker in town has decided to go out for the night and chosen the scummiest backstreet pub they can find to get pissed up in. The place is absolutely fucking heaving, standing room only. Just as well me and Dave got here early and bagged ourselves some seats in the corner, otherwise we'd be squashed up among them. We've got our feet up on some chairs opposite our table so we can save them for when Shaz and Dave's mates get here. We get a few funny looks from people standing nearby, but nobody says anything. They might be pissed up, but they're not fucking daft, yeah?

Dave's got his arms stretched out either side of him, resting on the back of the padded bench, tapping his fingers to the blaring Christmas music playing. It's not a band I've ever heard before, but they seem okay. They're a bit like the shouty skinhead bands Dave likes, except it's a bird singing and she's going on about snowmen and bollocks like that instead of kicking someone's head in at a football match. I've heard some of the songs before, I think they were originally done by dead people from the olden days, yeah? A few people nearby are shouting along in that tuneless way drunks do, waving their pints around and spilling half the contents down their reindeer jumpers. Me, I'm not at that stage yet, I've only had three pints of Guinness the whole fucking night, so I just wiggle my feet on the chair in time to the music.

"Who's this then?" I yell at Dave between songs.

"Vice Squad," he yells back. "They're an old punk band, my dad used to like them. It was him who got me into Oi when I were a kid."

"Yeah? So did they just do Christmas songs then?"

"Nah, they did all sorts. I'll download you a few mp3s, if you like them I'll get you everything else they did."

Dave's like that, he can get anything you want for free off his computer. Films, music, games for your phone, whatever you want. Fuck knows how he does it, I've never really been that interested in computers. We had them at school, but I could never get the hang of them. I bet Dave was some sort of fucking whizz-kid with them.

"Fucking Shaz is taking her time getting here," I yell, looking at the clock on my phone.

Dave shrugs and leans forward to pick up his lager. I put my phone away and shuffle myself upright on the bench, drop my feet to the floor. Some chancer standing nearby eyes up the vacant stool, so I glare at him to make sure he doesn't get any ideas about pinching it. He looks away, suitably traumatised, and I nod to myself in satisfaction.

"I'm going for a piss," I yell in Dave's ear. "Make sure no cunt pinches my seat."

Dave nods and raises a thumb, smiles at me in that lopsided way of his, then feels my arse as I climb over his legs. There's a brick wall of drunken people between me and the bogs, and it takes fucking ages to shove my way through them, so I'm nearly pissing myself by the time I get there. Luckily there's a spare cubicle so I dive into it and drop my knickers, then plonk my arse on the seat just in time. I kick the door closed with my foot and take out my phone, then turn on the camera and check my face. The bruises from my last fight are healing up quite well, so I should be good as new in a few more weeks. I switch off the camera and phone Shaz, ask her where the fuck she is. I can hear drunken singing in the background, so it's obvious she's not on her way here like she says she is. I tell her to fucking hurry up then, and put the phone away.

Back in the bar, this bloke in a Santa hat with a sprig of mistletoe sticking out of it stretches out his arms at me. "Bleuraaaaargh!" he says, or something like that, and lurches toward me for a Christmas kiss. I smile and duck under his arms, then skirt round him while he staggers forward into the space I just left. He spins round, looking confused. "Iss fuckern Crissmess, hen," he says, pointing at the mistletoe. "Iss the fuckern law." I give him two fingers and another smile, then fight my way back to Dave.

"About fucking time," Dave says. "I thought you'd fucked off or something."

"Nah," I say, and bend down to give him a quick snog. He tastes of cheese and onion crisps, and it makes me feel a bit hungry. I break away and sit down, then drain the rest of my Guinness. "You getting the drinks in then, or what?"

"Fucking hell Abby, I got the last round in."

"Yeah well, that makes you more experienced then doesn't it? Besides, it's what a fucking gentleman would do, isn't it?"

He grins at me and raises his eyebrows. "What, you think I'm a gentleman then?"

"Meh!" I say with a shrug, and he shuffles away into the crowd.

I suppose he is really, despite his rough as fuck outward appearance. Not in the traditional sense, like some fucking toff in a suit and tie or whatever, but he's definitely a gentle man. With me, anyway. Don't get me wrong, he's a fighter just like me, not some sort of fucking flower-loving softy. But he has his gentle side too, yeah? And he's not bothered if other blokes see it either. Most blokes I've been with act all macho when their mates are around, and treat me like some sort of fucking tart. Dave's not like that, he's different. I can't really explain it properly, it's just the way he is I guess.

I look up when I hear someone yelling my name. It's Shaz, standing by the door with Steve and Josh either side of her, holding her up with her arms draped over their shoulders. They're her boyfriends, yeah? Typical fucking Shaz, she has to go one better than me and have two of them. They're also Dave's mates, and they're both skinheads, just like him. Fuck knows what they get up to together, whether they take turns to fuck her or just take an end each or whatever, but they seem happy enough with the arrangement.

Shaz looks well and truly pissed up the way she staggers toward me, all three of them lurching to one side and bumping into people, spilling their drinks. Someone spins round yelling at them, then goes all shy and quiet when the two skinheads glare at him. They seem to have that effect on people, I don't know why. It's the same with Dave, I think it might be the clothes they wear or something. It's like people are afraid of them, yeah? But that's just fucking daft, they're just normal blokes. If you don't mess with them, they won't mess with you. Still, it seems to work to their advantage too, because people just clear a space for them when they see them coming. Like fucking what's-his-name from The Bible, the geezer who split the sea in half so his mates could walk through it.

Steve and Josh lower Shaz onto the bench next to me, then sit down on the two stools we saved for them. Shaz slumps against me. "Merry fucking humbug Abby," she says, breathing Pernod fumes in my face. "And a happy new whatsit, yeah?" She puts a hand over one eye and peers across the table at Josh. "Get the fucking drinks in, then. What you waiting for, a fucking message from the queen or something?"

Josh stands up and stretches out his braces. I notice he's got a twig of mistletoe sticking out of his crotch. Classy. I bet the bloke at the toilets wishes he'd thought of that.

Steve clasps his hands behind his head and grins at me. "All right, Abby?" he says. "How's the cage fighting going?"

"Yeah, not too bad," I say. "It pays the fucking bills anyway."

Which is true. Since I lost my job the fights have been my only means of income, yeah? Well except for the little bit extra I make with Shaz now and again, when the opportunity arises. But I haven't told Dave about that yet. Not because I don't think he would approve, he'd probably think it was funny as fuck. I just haven't got round to telling him yet.

"Steve, you cunt," Dave says when he gets back with a tray of drinks. He puts them down on the table one at a time, then slurps up the spillages from the tray. He's got three pints of Guinness for me, and four pints of lager for himself. He swears at Steve when he grabs one, but doesn't object when he takes a swig.

"What's all these for?" I ask, picking up one of the pints of Guinness.

"Thought it'd save time going to the bar later."

Good thinking. You see he's not just gentle, my Dave, he's fucking clever too. How lucky am I to have a bloke like that?

* * *

At chucking out time the streets are packed with people full of Christmas spirits, Christmas lager, Christmas whatever-gets-you-hammered. A gang of howling banshees stagger toward us in skimpy low-cut tops and mini-skirts, their high heels clattering on the vomit-soaked pavement. One points at Josh's mistletoe and laughs, then gets down on her knees and slobbers over his crotch while he just stands there grinning down at her. I clench my fists and look at Shaz, sure she'll want to steam in and batter the tart for messing with one of her boyfriends, and ready to help out if the others decide to join in. But Shaz is busy leaning over and puking into the gutter, and doesn't notice the assault on Josh's chastity. Steve is stood behind her, holding her hair out of the way so it doesn't get splattered with spew. Which is kind of a sweet thing to do, yeah? The sort of thing Dave would do for me if I had long hair like Shaz.

The banshees shuffle on, laughing and screeching at each other. A police car drives by slowly, and they all pull up their tops and wobble their tits at it. I can see the coppers inside smirking through the windscreen as they approach us. Dave glares at them as the car passes, then hacks up and spits into the road after it. Shaz straightens up, a line of bile dribbling down her chin. She wipes it away with the back of her hand and smiles at me.

"I fucking needed that," she says, while Steve gropes her tits from behind. She spins in his arms and grabs his arse, clamps her mouth onto his.

"Oi, what about me?" Josh asks.

Steve and Shaz break apart slightly to make room for him, and he buries his face in Shaz's tits, squashed between them as Steve and Shaz go back to sucking each other's mouths. I shake my head and sigh. Dave looks at me and shrugs, then moves toward me for a smooch of his own. I back up into a shop doorway, pulling Dave by his braces, so we won't get jostled by passing drunks. It stinks of piss and vomit, as I expected, but at least it's a bit more private. I've certainly been fingered in places a lot less romantic than this.

It's not long before we get interrupted by people shouting insults out in the street – fucking cunt, you wanker, come on then you bastards, things like that. At first we ignore it, it's not as if it's something unusual. People slagging each other off is just one of the Christmas traditions, yeah? Like decorating trees with tinsel and giving people you don't like crappy presents. But then the insults get a bit more personal and we realise who they are aimed at.

"You fucking baldy-headed cunts, call yourselves the fucking master race?"

Dave pulls his hand out of my knickers and spins round, steps out of the shop doorway with his fists clenched. "Fucking hell, another of the Nazi cunts," someone yells. "Let's fucking do the bastards." I rearrange my clothing and join Dave out on the pavement.

There's a bunch of middle-aged blokes waddling toward us in Santa hats, all beer guts and bravado. There's seven of them, and they're all driving fat fists into fat palms and grinning at each other like obese giant dwarfs who've just gang-banged Snow White. I catch Shaz's eye and smile. She smiles back and cracks her knuckles, first one hand, then the other. Dave, Steve and Josh line up before us like guardians protecting their princesses from an onslaught of barbarians. The Santas stop in the middle of the road and start up with their taunts again.

"Come on then, let's fucking have it," one says, beckoning with his fingers.

"We're going to fuck you up, real bad," another says, "just like we did with Hitler."

"Yeah," a third says, nodding his head so vigorously the white bobble on the end of his Santa hat smacks him in the face.

Dave, Steve and Josh just stand there looking at them, fists clenched, waiting for them to make a move. Shaz sighs. "For fuck's sake," she says, "what is this, a fucking internet flame war or something? Just get on with it, you fat bastards, or fuck off out of it."

"You fucking slag," one of the Santas yells, and rushes forward.

Steve and Josh both run forward to meet him. Josh gets there first and his fist disappears into Santa's blubbery stomach. Santa crumbles to his knees with an oof and Steve boots him in the face and sends him sprawling onto his back. The other Santas all roar and make a beeline for Josh, he being the shortest of the three skinheads they want to fuck up, and therefore the easiest-looking target. Dave wades in and kicks one up the arse, then spins round and smacks another in the mouth just as he's raising a fist to him.

Two Santas have got Josh held between them while a third sneers into his face, yelling something about Germany losing two world wars and one world cup. Fuck knows what that's got to do with anything, but Dave and Steve are both too busy with their own fights to see what's happening with Josh. Time to get out the big guns, yeah?

I look for Shaz, but she's already on her way. She snatches the Santa hats off the two fat blokes holding Josh, then grabs their hair and bangs their heads together. Josh kicks the other Santa in the bollocks mid-rant before he even realises what's happening. He bends over, clutching himself, and gets a knee in the face. I rush in to help Shaz with the two fat bastards when they turn toward her with their fists raised. Their fists hang there in the air as they stare at her, as if they don't know what to do with them.

Big fucking mistake, yeah?

I take one out with a quick jab of my fingers into his neck, followed by a punch to the chin that clacks his teeth together and sends blood spurting as he staggers backwards. Shaz knees hers in the bollocks, then drags him face down onto the tarmac by his hair. She kneels down on his back, then frisks his pockets and pulls out a wallet. He groans, so she punches him in the ear a few times until he shuts up, then stuffs his empty wallet into his mouth. She grins at me and waves a wad of cash, then gives me half and pockets the rest.

I look at Dave as I put the money away, inexplicably worried he might have seen what we just did. I'm not ashamed of it, it's just what we do now and again to make a bit of extra cash, yeah? But like I said, I haven't got round to telling him yet and I don't want him to find out this way. I needn't have worried though, Dave's too busy sticking the boot into one of the Santas rolling around in the road to notice what we're up to. I look around to see what the other Santas are doing, but they all seem to have legged it, so I wander over to Dave.

"You okay?" Dave asks when he sees me. He stops kicking the Santa and walks over to me, a concerned look on his face.

I shrug. "Yeah, why?"

"Sorry you had to see that."

"Don't be fucking daft. You were defending me and Shaz's honour, that's all. It's made me horny as fuck."

Dave grins. "Yeah?"

"Yeah. Now come on, before the fucking coppers get here. I don't want to spend Christmas in a fucking cell."

* * *

I lean over the edge of the multi-story car park wall and look down at the town centre below. There's fights all over the place as festivities continue without us, police and ambulance sirens wailing as they rush to each fresh incident. Coppers bash heads open while paramedics stitch them back together again and send them on to their next battle. So this is Christmas, yeah? That most fucking magical time of the year. Peace and good will to all men, except for whoever gets in your fucking way.

I snuggle up to Dave's chest, because it's fucking freezing up here. He puts his arm around me and draws me close, I listen to his heart beating and wonder when he's going to make his move. I hope he doesn't expect me to strip off up here, I don't think I'd be able to stop my teeth from chattering if he does. Shaz is already moaning away somewhere to my left, on her hands and knees with her arse in the air. You'd think Dave would have taken the hint by now, but he seems happy enough just watching the fights down below.

A church bell somewhere starts ringing, calling people in for midnight mass. I wonder if they have many fights in churches these days. If anyone even still goes to church. I haven't been since I was about five years old, and even then I thought it was boring as fuck.

"Happy birthday Jesus, you fucking hippy bastard!" Dave shouts. His voice echoes off nearby tower blocks.

The fighting in the town centre seems to stop all at once, as if someone's thrown a switch or something. Then there's sporadic drunken outbursts of that fucking Slade song coming from all directions. So here it is, merry fucking Christmas, yeah? Dave shrugs his arm off my shoulder and walks away a few steps. I get this rage of jealousy when I think he might be ogling Shaz's arse, or getting ideas about joining in with Steve and Josh. I don't know why, it just comes over me sometimes. I know it doesn't make any sense, but that's the way it is, yeah? But he's not even looking in their direction, he's facing the other way, fiddling with his jeans. Probably going to have a piss or something, and he's too shy to do it with me watching.

"You ready for your present yet?" he says, and spins round with his arms stretched out like Jesus on his stick. He's got his cock out, pointing it at me. But that's not what makes me smile. He's got a bit of ribbon tied round the middle of it, in a neat bow. Fuck knows where that's come from or where he learnt how to tie bows like that.

"Yeah," I say, and walk over to meet him. I kneel down and unwrap my present, give it a bit of a squeeze. "But this had better not be the only thing you've got me for Christmas or you're in some serious fucking shit."

Happy fucking Christmas, yeah?

Hank the Yank versus The Crips

or ... why Americans shouldn't try to write about British characters.

"Yee-Ha," Hank exclaimed, jumping off his horse in a single bound. "Time to get me some of them there faggots for my Christmas dinner." He tied his horse, Muffin, to an empty hitching post in the disabled area of the Tesco car park. "Y'all coming, Trixie?"

Trixie, still sitting in the passenger saddle at the back end of Muffin, looked down at Hank and shook her plastic grass pom-poms at him.

"Heck, Hank, what y'all doing parking old Muffin here in the disabled area for? We ain't got no disabilities, you dumb-arse."

Hank tilted back his ten-gallon hat and peered up at Trixie. He smiled. "Old Muffin here ain't as young as he used to be, so he ain't. Gonna be fit for the knacker's yard soon, I reckons. Besides, he started limping a bit while we crossed the prairie back yonder, I reckon he might've got bit by a rattlesnake or stepped on a cactus or somesuch. Reckon that makes him disabled enough for parking here, I surely do."

Trixie swung her leg over the saddle and jumped off the horse. Hank caught her in his arms and got a face-full of pom-poms for his trouble. He put her down and slapped her arse.

"Now go get me one of them there shopping trolleys. And make sure it ain't no wobbly one, you hear?"

"Y'all got a dollar coin on you for the trolley?" she asked.

Hank sighed and reached into his leather chaps for a dollar coin. He flipped it in the air and Trixie caught it in her mouth. She transferred both pom-poms to one hand and took the coin from her mouth, then inserted it into a nearby shopping trolley.

"Let's do this shit," she said, pushing the trolley into Tesco.

A tumbleweed drifted across the car park. Hank patted Muffin on the back and lit a cigar. "Y'all wait here while I mosey on down to that there Tesco and get me some faggots," he said to the horse. The horse nodded its head and whinnied.

A wrinkly old-timer standing at the Tesco entrance glared at Hank as he approached. He pointed at a *No Smoking* sign and shook his head.

God-damn health and safety laws, Hank thought. *God-damn government should get the God-damn hell out of my God-damn life.*

He stubbed out the cigar on the palm of his hand, smiling defiantly at the old-timer. The old-timer nodded and waved him through the door. Hank blew on his hand and shook it when he was out of sight.

Now look what your God-damn health and safety laws done gone and done to my God-damn hand.

He found Trixie by the gun department, shaking her pom-poms at a buy one get one free sign. He clumped toward her, his spurs clicking on the tiled floor as he walked. Trixie turned and smiled.

"Gimme a G," she chanted, thrusting up her left pom-pom. "Gimme a U." The right pom-pom shot above her head. "Gimme an N." The pom-poms swished past each other as Trixie crossed her arms above her head and dropped down to her knees. "Gimme some guns, motherfucker."

Hank shook his head slowly. "Hell, Trixie, ain't you got enough guns already? There's hardly enough space in our caravan as it is."

"A girl can never have too many guns," Trixie said. "What if there's another Apache uprising or our caravan gets surrounded by bears?"

"Heck, y'all know that ain't never gonna happen. The bears is all asleep for the winter, now. Besides, there ain't no picnic baskets at our caravan park to attract no bears, and all the Apaches are running bingo halls now so they ain't got no time for doing no uprising."

"But it's buy one get one free. Y'all know I can't resist a bargain like that. And it is Christmas Eve, and I bet you ain't done gone and bought my present yet."

Hank sighed. He never could resist Trixie's puppy-dog eyes, and it was true – he was planning to pick up a bottle of bath salts for her in Tesco while she wasn't looking. "Okay, but make them small ones, I don't want you filling up the shopping trolley with guns again like you did the last time they had a sale on. You gots to leave room for my faggots, ya hear?"

"You and your damn faggots," Trixie said, shaking her head. But at least she was smiling again.

Hank watched Trixie pull a couple of pink Uzi submachine guns from the shelf and plonk them in the shopping trolley. He sighed. "Shit Trixie, I said small ones."

"What?" Trixie asked. "They're smaller than the M60s, and they've got them in my colour. Now I just need to find some pink bullets for them and we're all set."

Trixie reached up, standing on her tippy-toes, but couldn't quite reach the boxes of pink ammunition on the top shelf. She beckoned Hank over and told him to assume the position. Hank bent down before her and clutched the back of his knees. Trixie climbed onto his back and swiped boxes off the shelf with her pom-poms. She jumped down and spun in a pirouette, then picked up the boxes and tossed them in the shopping trolley.

"Now can we go get me some damn faggots?" Hank asked, rubbing the base of his spine where Trixie's high heels had dug into him.

"Reckon you deserve them, honey, I surely do," Trixie said.

Hank led the way to the faggot section of the supermarket. They had his favourite, a pack of four Mr Brain's God-damn Great Faggots, but the Tesco own-brand

Super Saver Faggots next to them came in a pack of six for the same price. He picked up both packs and weighed them in his hands. Nothing much in it, but the Tesco brand was slightly heavier.

"Y'all going to be long?" Trixie asked. "Only I want to get back to the caravan park so I can try out my new guns."

"Yeah," Hank said absentmindedly while he studied the ingredients on the Tesco pack.

Trixie pointed. "Why don't you get those instead? They gots a special offer on."

Hank looked up. *Uncle Stan's Pukka Faggots*, a sign above the shelf read. *Buy two, throw one away.*

"Yee-Ha," Hank shouted, putting the two packs of faggots back on the shelf. He picked up six packs of Uncle Stan's Pukka Faggots and tossed them into the shopping trolley.

"Y'all ain't never gonna eat that many damn faggots," Trixie said, frowning.

"Shit girl," Hank said, "that don't matter. Look how much money we're saving. Now let's get this shit over to the till and get out of here before Old Muffin gets his britches in a tizzy thinking we gone done and left him."

Trixie pushed the shopping trolley to the till. Hank followed her and watched as she put their goods on a conveyor belt. A spotty kid working the till picked up one of the pink Uzi submachine guns and turned it around in his hands, looking for a barcode to scan. When he couldn't find one he put it down and reached under the till for a picture card showing different varieties of guns. He found the picture that matched Trixie's gun and scanned a barcode printed beneath it. Then he picked up the second gun and searched for a barcode on it.

"It's the same damn gun," Hank said, getting impatient. "Y'all just need to scan the same damn picture twice."

"And it's buy one get one free," Trixie added. "So don't go ripping us off none, y'hear?"

The kid looked up and nodded. He scanned the barcode

printed below the picture again and picked up a box of ammunition. Trixie stuffed the two Uzi submachine guns into the waistband of her rah-rah skirt and flounced out of the door. The kid scanned the remaining boxes of ammunition, then Hank's faggots. As Hank handed over his credit card, Trixie came running back into Tesco.

"It's the damn Crips," she yelled, waving her pom-poms. "They's coming across the prairie and they's headed straight for us."

"Hell, that's all we damn well need," Hank said. He put the faggots in one carrier bag and the boxes of ammunition in another, then headed for the door.

"Gimme my bullets, quick," Trixie said, dropping her pom-poms.

Hank reached into a carrier bag and held out a box of ammunition. Trixie snatched it from him and tore the box open with her teeth. She pulled out a handful of pink bullets and slapped them into one of the guns.

"Y'all want the other gun?" she asked.

Hank looked at the pink gun she held out for him and shook his head. "Hell no, I ain't no damn sissy boy."

Trixie grunted and loaded the other gun. She held one in each hand and stepped out into the car park. Hank picked up her pom-poms and stuffed them into one of the carrier bags and followed her out.

The old-timer at the door pointed frantically at a *No Loaded Guns* sign. Trixie barged past him and ran up to a parked wagon nearby. Its horse whinnied and reared up, but couldn't pull away because the wagon's handbrake was on. Hank glanced at Muffin, who had his nose in a water trough, and joined Trixie behind the wagon.

In the distance, Hank saw clouds of dust churned up on the prairie. As they got closer he could make out sitting figures, their hands frantically spinning large wheels by their sides. It was the damn Crips, all right. The most feared gang in all of Americaland, and here they were heading straight towards them.

"Oh, hell no," Hank said.

"Hell yeah," Trixie said, grinning. She stepped out from behind the wagon and raised her guns. "Eat pink leaden death, motherfuckers," she yelled.

Crips jerked and danced under her barrage of bullets. Wheelchairs spun out of control and tipped over. Trixie laughed, her arms juddering from the recoil of her pink submachine guns.

The Crips skidded to a halt and crouched behind their fallen comrades. One pulled out a bazooka and rested it over his shoulder, the barrel pointing straight at Trixie. Trixie was having too much fun to notice.

"Get the hell down," Hank yelled, but Trixie couldn't hear him over the roar of her twin guns. He ran out and grabbed her around the waist, then threw her onto the ground just as the bazooka flashed. The Crip's wheelchair shot backwards. The bazooka's shell whistled past Hank's head and exploded in the Tesco doorway. The old-timer standing there flew into the air and landed on the shop's roof. He glared down and shook his fist at Hank and Trixie.

The Crips were on the move again. Trixie shouted something, but Hank couldn't hear it over the ringing in his ears. She scrabbled across the ground to the two carrier bags he had left behind the wagon and rifled inside them. She pulled out a new box of ammunition and loaded her guns. The bazooka flashed once more and the wagon shattered into a thousand burning splinters of wood flying in the air. The horse ran away, its tail on fire. Trixie levelled her guns on the Crip with the bazooka and blew his head off.

"Yee-ha," Hank shouted. Another Crip raised a gun and fired at him. Hank's ten-gallon hat flew off his head. "God damn it," Hank said, and crawled after his hat. When he picked it up there was a bullet hole in both sides. "Oh, you're gonna pay for that, you God-damn bastard." Hank ran to Trixie's side and snatched one of the pink submachine guns from her hand. He pointed it at the remaining Crips and squeezed the trigger, swaying the gun from side to side as he watched them slump in their wheelchairs.

"Mighty fine shooting, partner," Trixie said when all the Crips lay still. "I reckon you gone and done deserved those faggots of yours now."

Hank nodded and gave Trixie her submachine gun back. She spun both guns over her fingers by the trigger guards as they walked back to Muffin.

"Oi, what about me?" the old-timer shouted down from the roof.

Hank looked up and tipped his hat at the old man. "You can buy your own God-damn faggots, we's out of here, y'all."

Also available from Marcus Blakeston

Punk Faction

Yorkshire punks Colin, Brian and Stiggy are looking forward to seeing top London Oi band The Cockney Upstarts when they play nearby. But a few days before the gig a simple misunderstanding with one of the local skinheads soon escalates into an all-out war. The Cockney Upstarts are much loved by both punks and skinheads alike, but is that enough to make them forget their differences for just one night?

Skinhead Away

A ska festival draws thousands of skinheads from across the country to the sleepy seaside town of Cleethorpes. Local residents and day-trippers look on in horror as the town is taken over by shaven-headed masses wearing boots and braces. But much to their surprise, the weekend unfolds peacefully. That is, until a group of drunken bikers think it would be a good laugh to smash up a few scooters, thinking they must belong to mods. Revenge is swift and vicious, but the bikers have friends too. Friends who are more than eager to settle the score.

Stabby Abby in ... Bare Knuckle Bitch

Best friends Abby and Shaz like nothing more than sticking the boot into some mug after a night out on the piss. That look of sheer terror on the bloke's face when he first realises what's coming his way. The way he begs for mercy right up until the moment he loses consciousness. It's the best buzz ever. The money in their wallets is just a bonus, a means to an end. Men are just walking pricks with money there for the taking. Treat them as anything else and they'll walk all over you.

Punk Rock Nursing Home

With the thirtieth anniversary of the death of 1980s prime minister Margaret Thatcher coming up in just a few weeks, Colin Baxter decides to make this year's Thatcher Day celebration something to be remembered. He contacts octogenarian punk band Sick Bastard and books them to play live at the retirement home, promising to pay them in free beer. There's just one problem: how to get the band, their equipment, and the beer, past the Gestapo retirement home manager who lives upstairs?

Runaway

Vegan anarcho punk Stiggy tags along with his mates to see top London Oi! band The Cockney Upstarts play their first ever northern gig at The Marples. He expects trouble when he sees all the skinheads who have turned up, but what he doesn't expect is to meet Sally, the girl of his dreams. There's just one problem – she's a skinhead too, and her boyfriend is absolutely massive. He's also ten years older than Stiggy, and very protective of his bird.

Mama Mia

In 1973, 99% of Earth's population are wiped out in an alien invasion. Satan's Bastards are among the 1% who survive. Holing up in a nature reserve at the arse end of nowhere, the men spend the next five years partying while their women scavenge for food and booze from the ruins of nearby towns and cities. But when a supply run goes tits up, it sets in motion a chain of events that will change their lives forever.

It's now 1978, and it's time for the mamas and old ladies of Satan's Bastards to fight back against the alien scum who wrecked their lives.

This is their story ...

Meadowside

Kylie and her friends from the council estate are shoplifting in Sportswear Direct when the Meadowside Shopping Centre is invaded by thousands of crazed killers with a taste for human flesh. Fighting to survive, she must choose who is most likely to be able to save her — an off duty policewoman, an aging skinhead in his sixties, or a psychotic football hooligan with a chainsaw.

Printed in Great Britain
by Amazon

Christmas at the Punk Rock Nursing Home

Christmas Eve 2043. Thatcher has been kidnapped by The Gestapo. Can the elderly residents of the Punk Rock Nursing Home rescue her in time to save Christmas?

Stabby Abby in ... A Very Stabby Xmas

Christmas Eve 2010. Best mates Abby and Shaz are out for a night on the piss with their blokes when they are accosted by a mob of drunken Santas.

ISBN 9781973497813